# Baa Baa Black Sheep

Retold by MEGAN BORGERT-SPANIOL

Illustrated by ANNIE WILKINSON

## CANTATA
LEARNING
MANKATO, MINNESOTA

CANTATA
LEARNING
MANKATO, MINNESOTA

Published by Cantata Learning
1710 Roe Crest Drive
North Mankato, MN 56003
www.cantatalearning.com

Library of Congress Control Number: 2014938272
ISBN: 978-1-63290-072-2

*Baa Baa Black Sheep* retold by Megan Borgert-Spaniol
Illustrated by Annie Wilkinson

Book design by Tim Palin Creative
Music produced by Wes Schuck
Audio recorded, mixed, and mastered at Two Fish Studios, Mankato, MN

Printed in the United States of America.

VISIT
WWW.CANTATALEARNING.COM/ACCESS-OUR-MUSIC

4

Sheep have soft **wool** that grows all year long. In spring, farmers **shear** their sheep. Then they wash the **fleece** and spin it into **yarn**!

When you hear the sheep baa, turn the page.

Baa baa black sheep, have you any wool?

Yes, sir, yes, sir, three bags full.

One for my **master**, one for my **dame**,

One for the little boy who lives down the lane.

Baa baa black sheep, have you any wool?

Yes, sir, yes, sir, three bags full.

Baa baa white sheep, have you any wool?

Yes, sir, yes, sir, three bags full.

11

One for my master, one for my dame,

One for the little boy who lives down the lane.

Baa baa white sheep, have you any wool?

Yes, sir, yes, sir, three bags full.

Baa baa gray sheep, have you any wool?

Yes, sir, yes, sir, three bags full.

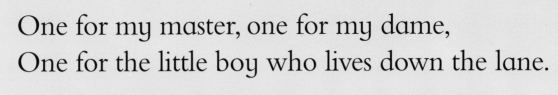

One for my master, one for my dame,
One for the little boy who lives down the lane.

Baa baa gray sheep, have you any wool?

Yes, sir, yes, sir, three bags full.

18

Baa baa black sheep, have you any wool?

Yes, sir, yes, sir, three bags full.

# GLOSSARY

**dame**—a woman in charge

**fleece**—the wool that is sheared from a sheep

**master**—a person who owns an animal

**shear**—to cut the wool off a sheep

**wool**—the thick, soft hair that grows on sheep

**yarn**—a long, thin material used to make clothing

# Baa Baa Black Sheep

Public Domain
Traditional

# TO LEARN MORE

Blair, Eric. *The Boy Who Cried Wolf: A Retelling of Aesop's Fable*. Mankato, MN: Picture Window Books, 2012.

Longenecker, Theresa. *Who Grows Up on the Farm?: A Book About Farm Animals and Their Offspring*. Minneapolis: Picture Window Books, 2003.

Schubert, Leda. *Feeding the Sheep*. New York: Farrar, Straus and Giroux, 2010.

Schuh, Mari C. *Sheep on the Farm*. Mankato, MN: Pebble Books, 2002.

Trapani, Iza. *Baa Baa Black Sheep*. Watertown, MA: Whispering Coyote, 2001.